God

Knows Your Name

Kim E. Douglas

ISBN 978-1-0980-2705-6 (paperback)
ISBN 978-1-0980-0632-7 (hardcover)
ISBN 978-1-0980-0633-4 (digital)

Christian Faith Publishing, Inc.
832 Park Avenue
Meadville, PA 16335
www.christianfaithpublishing.com

Printed in the United States of America

God Knows Your Name

Did you know that God knows your name?

Did you know that He can talk to you? That God can call you by your name?

In the Bible, God talked to a lot of people in different ways. But a few people he called by their name two times.

Let's find out who they were…

Abraham and Isaac

God spoke to Abraham through the voice of an angel from Heaven.

God called out, "Abraham, Abraham!"

"Here I am," said Abraham.

Genesis 22: 11–12

Isaac and Jacob

Later, Isaac had a son named Jacob.

So that means that Jacob was Abraham's grandson.

Jacob was thinking about going to Egypt. But Jacob was afraid.

5

Jacob

Then God spoke to him in a vision at night and said, "Jacob, Jacob."

"Here I am," Jacob replied.

A vision is like a dream. Do you ever dream?

God told Jacob not to be afraid to go to Egypt.

Genesis 46: 2–4

Jacob and His Family

Then Jacob and his family went to Egypt.

Genesis 46: 5–7

Moses

A lot of years later, God called another man. His name was Moses.

This time God's voice came from a burning bush.

Moses was a shepherd and was out in the desert taking care of sheep.

God spoke from the burning bush. "Moses, Moses!"

What do you think Moses said back to God?

Moses said, "Here I am."

Exodus 3:1–4

Samuel

So far, we've learned that God spoke to grown up men.

But did you know that God also speaks to kids just like you?

There was a special kid in the Bible that God spoke to, and his name was Samuel.

One night, Samuel was in his bed.

Then he heard a voice call his name. "Samuel, Samuel."

Then he heard the voice a second time. "Samuel, Samuel."

He heard the voice a third time. "Samuel, Samuel."

Then Samuel finally said, "Here I am. Speak, Lord, I am listening."

Wow! God called people by their name in the early days of the Bible.

I Samuel 3:1–10

Mei Zehn

We just learned that when God spoke to people, He called them by name.

God called out to Abraham through the voice of an angel…

God spoke to Jacob through a vision…

God spoke to Moses through a burning bush…

God called the little boy Samuel too!

José

Remember, God knows your name! Has God called your name?

Listen closely. Keep your ears and heart open.

God may call your name while you are sleeping.

Olivia

God may call your name when you are at home playing.

Olivia & Her Family

He may call your name when you are sitting quiet in a room with your family.

Victor

God wants to talk to you. So when He calls your name, be ready to answer!

Window is open, it is night, sky is bright and the voice of God speaks from Heaven and the voice calls Victor.

"Victor, Victor."

"Here I am Lord. I am listening."

The Beginning…